This Time, Tempe Wick?

This Time, Tempe Wick?

Patricia Lee Gauch

Margot Tomes

Boyds Mills Press

Text copyright © 1974, 2002
Illustrations copyright © 1974, 2002
All rights reserved

Published by Boyds Mills Press, Inc.
A Highlights Company
815 Church Street, Honesdale, Pennsylvania 18431
Printed in China

Publisher Cataloging-in-Publication Data (U.S.)
Gauch, Patricia Lee.
This time, Tempe Wick? / by Patricia Lee Gauch ; illustrated by Margot Tomes.
[48] p. : col. ill. ; cm.
Originally published: N.Y.: Coward, McCann & Geoghegan, Inc., 1974.
Summary: Everyone knows Tempe Wick is a most surprising girl, but she exceeds even her own reputation
when two mutinous U.S. Revolutionary War soldiers try to steal her beloved horse.
ISBN 1-59078-179-1 (hc)   ISBN 1-59078-185-6 (pbk)
1. United States—History—Revolution, 1775–1783—Juvenile fiction. 2. Pennsylvania History—
Revolution, 1775–1783 Juvenile fiction. (1. United States History—Revolution, 1775–1783—Fiction. 2.
Pennsylvania History—Revolution, 1775–1783—Fiction. 3. Horses—Fiction.)
I. Tomes, Margot, ill. II. Title.
[F] 21   PZ7.G2315Th 2003
2003100690
First Boyds Mills Press edition, 2003

10 9 8 7 6 5 4 3 2 1 HC
10 9 8 7 6 5 4 3 2 1 PB

For Mary Christine

Long ago, when this country was just going about the business of being born, there lived in a little brown farmhouse in the Jersey hollows a most surprising girl named Temperance Wick.

Tempe, she was called.

And she was surprising for that many reasons. She surprised her mother because she didn't stop growing when other girls did.

She went right on—inch by inch—growing up and out until some people said she looked more like the Wicks' bull Joshua than either her mother or her father.

She surprised her friend David because when they wrestled she could toss him halfway across the Wick kitchen two out of three times.

She surprised her father because she could stay at the plow as long as he on a spring night, and she could beat him in a race across Jockey Hollow on her horse Bonny from the time she was nine.

Everyone, up the pike to Morristown, across the hills to Mendham, all the way to the swamps of Green Village, knew that Tempe Wick was a surprising girl.

But no one knew just how surprising until the middle of the American Revolution when Tempe got mad. Storming, had-quite-enough mad!

Then everyone—up the pike to Morristown, across the hills to Mendham, all the way to the swamps of Green Village—found out that Tempe could be most surprising. And clever as well!

Now, it took a good deal to make Tempe Wick that mad even during those troubled days.

She and her mother and father and her grown-up brothers and sisters had all wanted America to be free from the British king and all his rules. So in 1779 when General George Washington himself asked if his American troops might winter in Jockey Hollow, the Wicks and their neighbors said yes.

That didn't make Tempe mad at all.

More than ten thousand men came to Jockey Hollow. They built so many cabins in the hills around the hollow that the once-empty woods looked like a log city. They built a hospital and a kitchen, and they practiced shooting on the very spot where Tempe and her horse Bonny once raced.

That didn't make Tempe mad either.

In fact, she and her mother and father wanted freedom from the British so much, they helped. They shared the wheat they grew, the cows they fattened. Even after Tempe's father died and her mother got sick, Tempe went on helping. She knitted and cooked and sewed to help the tattered soldiers get through the bitter, blizzardy winters.

That certainly didn't make her mad.

No, it wasn't until New Year's night of 1781 that Tempe got so mad and so surprising (and clever as well).

It started late that night. The moon had spilled over the snow-patched hills like a silver stream. The wind moaned through the creaky limbs. Inside the Wick house Tempe and her mother were alone. Tempe was buried under three feather quilts fast asleep. Her mother, too, after having coughed and coughed and coughed, had finally fallen asleep.

But across the orchard and over the hill at the soldiers' camp, no one was asleep. The soldiers from Pennsylvania were nearly the only soldiers still camped there and they had been growing more and more unhappy lately. They had not had enough food to keep their stomachs half-filled. They had almost no blankets, and they had not been paid for a year.

At first they only downed their New Year's whiskey and shouted angrily around their huts. Then they started blasting their muskets into the air. Finally, they stormed across the Wick

orchard, captured the cannons, and told their officers, "We quit!"

It was a mutiny.

And the Wick house sat nearly in the middle of it.

Tempe wasn't at all sure what was going on. When, half-asleep, she heard the shouting, she pulled the quilts over her head and wondered how long the party would go on. When the shots exploded, she put the pillow over her head, too, and hoped the party would end soon. But when the cannon went off, she jumped out of bed, grabbed her rifle, and said, "The British have come!"

It was the camp blacksmith who ran by and told her otherwise.
"It's a mutiny, ma'am. Take cover," said the blacksmith.
"From our own soldiers, sir?" said she.

"Aye. They're agin their own captains. They're agin their own general. They may be agin you! You've food to fill their stomachs and a horse to get them away. That's reason enough!"

And off he ran.

He didn't even see Tempe get mad. But she did.

"Agin me!" she said to herself, pushing up the sleeves of her nightgown. "Agin me, indeed! I've shared the wheat from my fields, sir, and the cows from my herd. And I do not see how it will serve their war to make a war on me. But if any soldier takes from my home or steals from my barn or tries to take my Bon . . . he'll have to battle me first!"

And she loaded her rifle, poked it through a small crack in the kitchen window, and vowed not to move from the spot until every soldier was off her farm.

And she kept her word. Until just after midnight. Then a thousand soldiers, followed by one general, marched off to Philadelphia to tell the leaders of all America how they were hungry and cold and poor. As they passed, the men shouted. The fifers fifed. The drummers drummed, but when the cannoneer fired off his cannon three times, the very windows in the Wick house rattled and Mrs. Wick woke up and started to cough.

Nor was it an ordinary cough. Mrs. Wick coughed until her ears flushed pink. She coughed until the bed shook. She coughed and coughed and coughed.

And Tempe knew she couldn't stay put. Her mother needed medicine and only Dr. William had it. At daybreak, soldiers or no soldiers, she would have to leave the house. She would have to get to the barn and ride Bonny down the trail to the doctor's farm.

It was then she learned that all the soldiers had not gone to Philadelphia. Soldiers were everywhere. Some were still celebrating in the cornfield. Some were sleeping against the smokeshed. Others were at the well.

But Tempe went anyway, and she didn't go shouting and she didn't go shooting. Not this time. After hiding her mother in the cellar she bundled up in her Sunday coat and fine hat and walked . . . slowly . . . to the barn, just as if she were alone in the world. She pretended not to see the soldier peeking through the fence at her. She pretended not to see the soldier duck up into the loft.

She whistled a little tune and went right to Bonny's stall and coolly and calmly and casually put on her bridle and saddle and rode, coolly and calmly and casually, right past them all. It was as if she were the white-horse lead in a military parade.

The soldiers just watched.

Not until she got to the road did she hurry. Then she touched her Bon with a stick and raced down the road to Dr. William's. It had all been so easy. Probably, she thought, those soldiers didn't want anything from the Wicks at all. Probably the blacksmith had been just the smallest bit nervous.

But when she left Dr. William's with a full bottle of medicine, she learned differently. Out of the thicket, right in front of the doctor's house, jumped two soldiers.

Even Tempe's stomach took a flip.

"Pretty young lady," said the one, "that's a fine horse you have."

"Thank you, sir." She smiled and started by.

But the other, a thin man with sideburns that curled like an *S* around his ears, stopped her.

"I imagine a fine mare like that could carry me and my friend, say, all the way to Philadelphia," he said.

"I imagine," Tempe said, and tried to get by again.

"Then, we'll try her now!" he said and quickly grabbed the reins from Tempe. "Get down!"

Tempe didn't even blink. Not this time. She turned her head, coyly, so sweetly, so perfectly, and said, "But sir, 'tis my best horse Bon."

"Then she'll do her best for us. Get down I say." He was terribly gruff.

But Tempe was not. She said, still coyly and sweetly and perfectly, "Then perhaps you will help me down, sir."

And, frowning, he reached to help, but as he did, Tempe snatched the reins back, put a stick to Bon's hide, and raced off down the lane toward the Wick farm.

"Come on, speeder," she whispered as she hung on Bon's neck.

Both of the soldiers started running after them. The one fired a shot. BAM! But it merely sent Bonny flying faster and faster and faster down the road. Her nostrils steamed and her hooves pounded so fast, they barely touched the ground. The clickety-clackety sounded more like a gentle rain on the frozen road.

All of the other soldiers were gone when Tempe rode up under the willow that guarded the back door, but she didn't lead Bonny back to the barn. That would be too easy. She didn't try to squeeze Bonny in the smokeshed. She'd quickly be found. Nor did Tempe even hide Bon in the woods. The soldiers knew the woods well.

No, Tempe did a most surprising thing. She led Bonny right in the back door and into the kitchen of the Wick house.

Of course Tempe didn't tie her there. Everyone visited the kitchen first, particularly when the blizzards whipped around the Wick house in January. Tempe led Bon straight through the

sitting room, too. Old Bon might not treat kindly her Grandmother Wick's fine desk from England or her mother's favorite fiddleback chair. And Tempe's mother's cough was not apt to improve with a horse sharing her bedroom!

So Tempe took the mare into her own room, the tiny dark room with the two tiny windows in the back of the house, where she left her, happily nibbling at the flax-woven spread on Tempe's bed.

And just in time, for Tempe had just brought her mother up from the cellar when there came a terrible thumping on the back door.

It was the man with the curled sideburns. He bellowed through the crack in the door, "I want that gray mare!"

But Tempe answered lazily, as if she had been spinning wool all afternoon, "A gray mare, sir? Have you lost one?"

Well, the man and his friend didn't even reply. They stalked off across the kitchen garden. Tempe scratched a peekhole in the frosted window just big enough to see them stomp into the barn. They sent the cow out mooing. They sent chickens out flying. And hay tumbled out of the loft like a dust storm in January

when they searched there. Nor had they any better luck in the smokeshed or woods.

The soldiers, by now terribly red in the face, just returned to the Wick house long enough to promise, "We know she's here . . . somewhere, pretty lady. And we intend to wait until we find her!"

Wait?

Even Tempe was surprised at that! How long could she hide a horse in her bedroom?

But Tempe didn't worry long. Not this time. For now, her house was her fort. For later, perhaps the general and his men would come back from Philadelphia and capture the runaway soldiers. Perhaps Dr. William would drop by to see how her mother was faring and run the soldiers off. Perhaps with a healthy dose of medicine her mother could help. Two against two were happier odds. Or perhaps the two soldiers would just go away by themselves.

Satisfied with all the possibilities, Tempe stayed at her window post until dark. Then she curled up on the kitchen settle (having a guest in her bedroom) and went to sleep.

But the next morning the general and his men were not back from Philadelphia. There was no sight of Dr. William. The medicine had stopped Mrs. Wick's cough, but it had also made

her sleep and sleep and sleep. And the two soldiers were still there, already pacing the barnyard.

To make things worse, Bonny was hungry.

First she just walked angry circles around Tempe's bed. Then she started thumping her hoof at the door. Finally she let out a "Whiiiiiiinnnnnnnnyyyyyyy!" that Tempe was sure could be heard all the way to the barn.

Tempe knew Bonny had to be fed.

She bundled herself up and headed into the north wind toward the barn.

She quickly fed the other animals, then stacked both arms full of hay and was about to return when a voice boomed down at her from the loft.

"Ah—ha!" It was the soldier with the curled sideburns. "Where are you going with the hay, miss?" he asked.

"To the house, sir," Tempe answered lightly. "My mother is ill and last night the wind blew through the cracks in our roof like a gale of ice. The hay will stop up the cracks."

The soldier grumbled something quietly and to himself, but he let her pass.

All day the two soldiers hovered around the barnyard, and there was nothing for Tempe to do but wait. Yet little happened. Her mother slept on and on. The general did not come, nor did Dr. William. And while the hay promised to last another day, Tempe saw the little water she had for Bonny was quickly disappearing.

In the morning it was gone. Bonny grew so thirsty she licked the frost off the window. She licked Tempe's washbowl dry, and finally she whinnied, this time so loudly Tempe was sure, had the soldiers been in Jockey Hollow, they would have heard her!

Bonny had to be watered.

When Tempe had drawn three buckets at the well, both soldiers stepped up behind her.

"May we help, pretty lady?" said the one.

"No, thank you, sir," said she. "I go only to the house, and I am quite able." She balanced one bucket under her arm and gripped two in her hands.

"You must be very thirsty," said the other. "Why, there is enough water there for a horse!"

Tempe smiled. "Perhaps," she said, "but these bucketfuls are to scrub my floors. It is said a fierce winter is followed by an early spring, and I am but preparing for that. But I thank you."

She curtsied slightly and started toward the door.

Again the soldiers grumbled, but let her pass.

On the third day Tempe had stopped looking for anyone to come to help. The soldiers had moved closer to the house, and she was worried about Bonny.

Bon didn't circle the bed or thump the door, and she let loose only the tiniest whinny. Tempe barely heard it in the kitchen. But that is what worried Tempe.

"Bonny's spirits are low," Tempe said to her mother, who was still half-asleep. "She must need oats."

That morning Tempe fed the hog and the cows and the sheep as usual. Then she began to gather her oats. She put some in her pockets. She stuffed more in her bag, and she filled her bucket to brimful, then started back. The soldiers were waiting by the gate when she passed.

"Surely," said the one, looking in the bucket, "you don't eat unground oats, my dear."

"Oh, yes," said Tempe, walking on. "Boiled, they make a fine porridge."

"But," said the one, following her, "so many oats for two ladies, and one so ill?"

"It is barely enough," said Tempe. "Some days, after chores, I eat three bowls at one sitting."

Still he followed.

"Some days," Tempe went on, "I eat four!"

He was at the door in front of her.

"Next to applesauce with brown sugar, I crave oats most!" she said, looking directly into his eyes. "These will last only a day."

"Just the same," said the soldier, "I begin to think there is a third lady in the house. A gray mare that can race like the wind. And I wish to see for myself."

With that, the one soldier pushed right past Tempe into the house. He stomped into the kitchen, knocking the pots off the table and the wood across the floor. He stomped into the pantry, shaking the jars from the shelf.

Then he heard the slightest whinny—or was it a cough?—
and he stomped through the sitting room toward the bedroom,
brushing the ink from Grandmother's desk and finally tipping
over Mrs. Wick's favorite fiddleback chair.

But that was one push too many. And this time Tempe didn't
just get mad, she got storming, had-quite-enough mad, and she
began to look a good bit like the Wicks' bull Joshua.

'That," she said—neither coyly, nor sweetly, nor perfectly—
"was my mother coughing. But if it were a herd of gray horses

feeding on my bed, I would not let you through that door, smash-and breaking.”

The soldier scoffed and went for the cellar door.

Tempe was there first. “Not into the cellar, sir.”

He darted for the attic door.

Tempe beat him there, too. “Not into the attic.”

He eyed the bedroom door again.

“Not anywhere,” she said.

And before the soldier had time to doubt it, Tempe kicked open the front door with one foot, kicked his musket out of his hand with the other—and pushed him, right out the doorway.

For a moment—was it two?—the soldier lay sprawled on the path, glaring at Tempe, his face reddening around his curled sideburns. But Tempe stood firm in the doorway with *his* musket in *her* hand and glared back.

Finally, he picked up his hat and paced to his friend at the fence where they huddled, then started—on foot—down the road to Pennsylvania. At last they disappeared.

It was a half day later when everything left to happen happened, all at once. The general didn't come, but a colonel did. He came knocking at the door to say it appeared the Pennsylvania troops would be given back-money and clothes and food by the leaders in Philadelphia. Dr. William came to see how Mrs. Wick was. And with everyone standing at the front door, Mrs. Wick herself got up and said she felt much better, thank you, and would anyone like tea? And everyone said, yes, if you please.

Everyone . . . except Tempe, who said the cows needed hay, the pigs needed grain, the chickens needed water, and Bonny and she needed to get out of their "fort" for a long, quiet ride through the woods.

And after hearing her story, that wasn't surprising—not to the colonel or the doctor or her mother, not up the pike to Morristown, across the hills to Mendham, or all the way to Green Village—not surprising at all.

Author's Note

Tempe Wick was a real colonial girl whose tidy brown shingle house still stands the way it did 200 years ago on a quiet back road near Morristown, New Jersey.

The legend on which this story is based has been widely shared since the days Tempe and her horse raced the Jockey Hollow roads. Many historians have regarded it as true. They say she was indeed known for her strength and her nerve, and they claim as further proof the hoofprints of Tempe's horse, which remained on the bedroom floor until this very century, when a more recent owner replaced the battered boards.

Legend or no, however, the story is more than the events of a young woman and her pet horse as they lived through the Revolutionary War. War is never simple. A large war is made of many small wars, often among people who are fighting on the same side. Soldiers against soldiers. Soldiers against farmers. Farmers against soldiers. The Pennsylvania soldiers had been treated badly and forgotten during this period of the Revolutionary War, but when in their bitterness two of them tried to steal from a feisty farm girl, they found themselves faced with a war of a new kind.

Patricia Lee Gauch